The Cremona Violin

By

E. T. A. Hoffmann

British Library Cataloguing-in-Publication Data
A catalogue record for this book is available from
the British Library

Contents

E. T. A. HOFFMAN

Ernst Theodor Wilhelm Hoffmann was born in Königsberg, East Prussia in 1776. His family were all jurists, and during his youth he was initially encouraged to pursue a career in law. However, in his late teens Hoffman became increasingly interested in literature and philosophy, and spent much of his time reading German classicists and attending lectures by, amongst others, Immanuel Kant.

In was in his twenties, upon moving with his uncle to Berlin, that Hoffman first began to promote himself as a composer, writing an operetta called *Die Maske* and entering a number of playwriting competitions. Hoffman struggled to establish himself anywhere for a while, flitting between a number of cities and dodging the attentions of Napoleon's occupying troops. In 1808, while living in Bamberg, he began his job as a theatre manager and a music critic, and Hoffman's break came a year later, with the publication of *Ritter Gluck*. The story centred on a man who meets, or thinks he has met, a long-dead composer, and played into the 'doppelgänger' theme – at that time very popular in literature. It was shortly after this that Hoffman began to use the pseudonym E. T. A. Hoffmann, declaring the 'A' to stand for 'Amadeus', as a tribute to the great composer, Mozart.

Over the next decade, while moving between Dresden, Leipzig and Berlin, Hoffman produced a great range of both literary and musical works. Probably Hoffman's most well-known story, produced in 1816, is 'The Nutcracker and the Mouse King', due to the fact that – some seventy-six years later - it inspired Tchaikovsky's ballet *The Nutcracker.* In the same vein, his story 'The Sandman' provided both the inspiration for Léo Delibes's ballet *Coppélia,* and the basis for a highly influential essay by Sigmund Freud, called 'The Uncanny'. (Indeed, Freud referred to Hoffman as the "unrivalled master of the uncanny in literature.")

Alcohol abuse and syphilis eventually took a great toll on Hoffman though, and – having spent the last year of his life paralysed – he died in Berlin in 1822, aged just 46. His legacy is a powerful one, however: He is seen as a pioneer of both Romanticism and fantasy literature, and his novella, *Mademoiselle de Scudéri: A Tale from the Times of Louis XIV* is often cited as the first ever detective story.

The Cremona Violin

E. T. A. Hoffmann

(1776-1822)

Councillor Krespel was one of the strangest, oddest men I ever met with in my life. When I went to live in H— for a time the whole town was full of talk about him, as he happened to be just then in the midst of one of the very craziest of his schemes. Krespel had the reputation of being both a clever, learned lawyer and a skilful diplomatist. One of the reigning princes of Germany – not, however, one of the most powerful – had appealed to him for assistance in drawing up a memorial, which he was desirous of presenting at the Imperial Court with the view of furthering his legitimate claims upon a certain strip of territory. The project was crowned with the happiest success; and as Krespel had once complained that he could never find a dwelling sufficiently comfortable to suit him, the prince, to reward him for the memorial, undertook to defray the cost of building a house which Krespel might erect just as he pleased. Moreover, the prince was willing to purchase any site that he should fancy. This offer, however, the Councillor would not accept; he insisted that the house should be built in his garden, situated in a very beautiful neighbourhood outside the town walls. So he bought all kinds of materials and had them carted out. Then he might have been seen day after day, attired in his curious garments (which he had made himself according to certain fixed rules of his own), slacking the lime, riddling the sand, packing up the bricks and stones in regular heaps, and so on. All this he did without once consulting an architect or thinking about a plan. One fine day, however, he went to an experienced builder of the town and requested him to be in his garden at daybreak the next morning, with all his journeymen and apprentices, and a large body of labourers, &c., to build him his house. Naturally the builder asked for the architect's plan, and was not a little astonished when Krespel replied that none was needed, and that things would turn out all right in the end, just as he wanted them. Next morning, when the builder and his

4

men came to the place, they found a trench drawn out in the shape of an exact square; and Krespel said, 'Here's where you must lay the foundations; then carry up the walls until I say they are high enough.' 'Without windows and doors, and without partition walls?' broke in the builder, as if alarmed at Krespel's mad folly. 'Do what I tell you, my dear sir,' replied the Councillor quite calmly: 'leave the rest to me; it will be all right.' It was only the promise of high pay that could induce the builder to proceed with the ridiculous building; but none has ever been erected under merrier circumstances. As there was an abundant supply of food and drink, the workmen never left their work; and amidst their continuous laughter the four walls were run up with incredible quickness, until one day Krespel cried, 'Stop!' Then the workmen, laying down trowel and hammer, came down from the scaffoldings and gathered round Krespel in a circle, whilst every laughing face was asking, 'Well, and what now?' 'Make way!' cried Krespel; and then running to one end of the garden, he strode slowly towards the square of brick-work. When he came close to the wall he shook his head in a dissatisfied manner, ran to the other end of the garden, again strode slowly towards the brick-work square, and proceeded to act as before. These tactics he pursued several times, until at length, running his sharp nose hard against the wall, he cried, 'Come here, come here, men! break me a door in here! Here's where I want a door made!' He gave the exact dimensions in feet and inches, and they did as he bid them. Then he stepped inside the structure, and smiled with satisfaction as the builder remarked that the walls were just the height of a good two-storeyed house. Krespel walked thoughtfully backwards and forwards across the space within, the bricklayers behind him with hammers and picks, and wherever he cried, 'Make a window here, six feet high by four feet broad!' 'There a little window, three feet by two!' a hole was made in a trice.

It was at this stage of the proceedings that I came to H—; and it was highly amusing to see how hundreds of people stood round about the garden and raised a loud shout whenever the stones flew out and a new window appeared where nobody had for a moment expected it. And in the same manner Krespel proceeded with the buildings and fittings of the rest of the house, and with all the work necessary to that end; everything had to be done on the spot in accordance with the instructions which the Councillor gave from time to time. However, the absurdity of the whole business, the growing conviction that things would in the end turn out better than might have been expected, but above all, Krespel's generosity – which indeed cost him nothing – kept them all in good-humour. Thus were the difficulties overcome which necessarily arose out of this eccentric way of building, and in a short time there was a completely finished house, its outside, indeed, presenting a most extraordinary appearance, no two windows, &c., being alike, but on the other hand the interior arrangements suggested a peculiar feeling of comfort. All who entered the house bore witness to the truth of this; and I too experienced it myself when I was taken in by Krespel after I had become more intimate with him. For hitherto I had not exchanged a word with this eccentric man; his building had occupied him so much that he had not even once been to Professor M—'s to dinner, as he was in the habit of going on Tuesdays. Indeed, in reply to a special invitation, he sent word that he should not set foot over the threshold before the house-warming of his new building took place. All his friends and acquaintances, therefore, confidently looked forward to a great banquet; but Krespel invited nobody except the masters, journeymen, and labourers who had built the house. He entertained them with the choicest viands: bricklayer's apprentices devoured partridge pies regardless of consequences; young joiners polished off roast pheasants with the greatest success; whilst hungry labourers helped themselves for once to the choicest morsels of *truffes fricassées*. In the evening their wives and daughters came, and there was a great ball. After waltzing a short while with the wives of the masters, Krespel sat down amongst the town-musicians, took a violin in his hand, and directed the orchestra until daylight.

On the Tuesday after this festival, which exhibited Councillor Krespel in the character of a friend of the people, I at length saw him appear, to my no little joy, at Professor M—'s. Anything more strange and fantastic than Krespel's behaviour it would be impossible to find. He was so stiff and awkward in his movements, that he looked every moment as if he would run up against something or do some damage. But he did not; and the lady of the house seemed to be well aware that he would not, for she did not grow a shade paler when he rushed with heavy steps round a table crowded with beautiful cups, or when he manoeuvred near a large mirror that reached down to the floor, or even when he seized a flower-pot of beautifully painted porcelain and swung it round in the air as if desirous of making its colours play. Moreover, before dinner he subjected everything in the Professor's room to a most minute examination; he also took down a picture from the wall and hung it up again, standing on one of the cushioned chairs to do so. At the same time he talked a good deal and vehemently; at one time his thoughts kept leaping, as it were, from one subject to another (this was most conspicuous during dinner); at another, he was unable to have done with an idea; seizing upon it again and again, he gave it all sorts of wonderful twists and turns, and couldn't get back into the ordinary track until something else took hold of his fancy. Sometimes his voice was rough and harsh and screeching, and sometimes it was low and drawling and singing; but at no time did it harmonize with what he was talking about. Music was the subject of conversation; the praises of a new composer were being sung, when Krespel, smiling, said in his low singing tones, 'I wish the devil with his pitchfork would hurl that atrocious garbler of music millions of fathoms down to the bottomless pit of hell!' Then he burst out passionately and wildly, 'She is an angel of heaven, nothing but pure God-given music! – the paragon and queen of song!' – and tears stood in his eyes. To understand this, we had to go back to a celebrated *artiste,* who had been the subject of conversation an hour before.

Just at this time a roast hare was on the table; I noticed that Krespel carefully removed every particle of meat from the bones on his plate, and was most particular in his inquiries after the hare's feet; these the Professor's little five-year-old daughter now brought to him with a very pretty smile. Besides, the children had cast many friendly glances towards Krespel during dinner; now they rose and drew nearer to him, but not without signs of timorous awe. What's the meaning of that? thought I to myself. Dessert was brought in; then the Councillor took a little box from his pocket, in which he had a miniature lathe of steel. This he immediately screwed fast to the table, and turning the bones with incredible skill and rapidity, he made all sorts of little fancy boxes and balls, which the children received with cries of delight. Just as we were rising from table, the Professor's niece asked, 'And what is our Antonia doing?' Krespel's face was like that of one who has bitten of a sour orange and wants to look as if it were a sweet one; but this expression soon changed into the likeness of a hideous mask, whilst he laughed behind it with downright bitter, fierce, and as it seemed to me, satanic scorn. 'Our Antonia? our dear Antonia?' he asked in his drawling, disagreeable singing way. The Professor hastened to intervene; in the reproving glance which he gave his niece I read that she had touched a point likely to stir up unpleasant memories in Krespel's heart. 'How are you getting on with your violins?' interposed the Professor in a jovial manner, taking the Councillor by both hands. Then Krespel's countenance cleared up, and with a firm voice he replied, 'Capitally, Professor; you recollect my telling you of the lucky chance which threw that splendid Amati* into my hands. Well, I've only cut it open today – not before today. I hope Antonia has carefully taken the rest of it to pieces.' 'Antonia is a good child,' remarked the Professor. 'Yes, indeed, that she is,' cried the Councillor, whisking himself round; then, seizing his hat and stick, he hastily rushed out of the room. I saw in the mirror how that tears were standing in his eyes.

As soon as the Councillor was gone, I at once urged the Professor to explain to me what Krespel had to do with violins, and

*The Amati were a celebrated family of violin-makers of the sixteenth and seventeenth centuries, belonging to Cremona in Italy. They form the connecting-link between the Brescian school of makers and the greatest of all makers, Stradivarius and Guarnieri.

particularly with Antonia. 'Well,' replied the Professor, 'not only is the Councillor a remarkably eccentric fellow altogether, but he practises violin-making in his own crack-brained way.' 'Violin-making!' I exclaimed, perfectly astonished. 'Yes,' continued the Professor, 'according to the judgement of men who understand the thing, Krespel makes the very best violins that can be found nowadays; formerly he would frequently let other people play on those in which he had been especially successful, but that's been all over and done with now for a long time. As soon as he has finished a violin he plays on it himself for one or two hours, with very remarkable power and with the most exquisite expression, then he hangs it up beside the rest, and never touches it again or suffers anybody else to touch it. If a violin by any of the eminent old masters is hunted up anywhere, the Councillor buys it immediately, no matter what the price put upon it. But he plays it as he does his own violins, only once; then he takes it to pieces in order to examine closely its inner structure, and should he fancy he hasn't found exactly what he sought for, he in a pet throws the pieces into a big chest, which is already full of the remains of broken violins.' 'But who and what is Antonia?' I inquired, hastily and impetuously. 'Well, now, that,' continued the Professor, 'that is a thing which might very well make me conceive an unconquerable aversion to the Councillor, were I not convinced that there is some peculiar secret behind it, for he is such a good-natured fellow at bottom as to be sometimes guilty of weakness. When he came to H—, several years ago, he led the life of an anchorite, along with an old housekeeper, in – Street. Soon, by his oddities, he excited the curiosity of his neighbours; and immediately he became aware of this, he sought and made acquaintances. Not only in my house but everywhere we became so accustomed to him that he grew to be indispensable. In spite of his rude exterior, even the children liked him, without ever proving a nuisance to him; for notwithstanding all their friendly passages together, they always retained a certain timorous awe of him, which secured him against all over-familiarity. You have today had an example of the way in which he wins their hearts by his ready skill in various things. We all took him at first for a crusty old bachelor, and he never contradicted us. After he had been living here some time, he went away, nobody knew where, and returned at the end of some months. The evening following his return his windows were lit up to an unusual extent; this alone was sufficient to arouse his neighbours' attention, and they soon heard the surpassingly beautiful voice of a female singing to the accompaniment of a piano. Then the music of a violin was heard chiming in and entering upon a keen ardent contest with the voice. They knew at once that the player was the Councillor. I myself mixed in the large crowd which had gathered in front of his house to listen to this extraordinary concert; and I must confess that, beside this voice and the peculiar, deep soul-stirring impression which the execution made upon me, the singing of the most celebrated *artistes* whom I had ever heard seemed to me feeble and void of expression. Until then I had had no conception of such long-sustained notes, of such nightingale trills, of such undulations of musical sound, of such swelling up to the strength of organ-notes, of such dying away to the faintest whisper. There was not one whom the sweet witchery did not enthral; and when the singer ceased, nothing but soft sighs broke the impressive silence. Somewhere about midnight the Councillor was heard talking violently, and another male voice seemed, to judge from the tones, to be reproaching him, whilst at intervals the broken words of a sobbing girl could be detected. The Councillor continued to shout with increasing violence, until he fell into that drawling, singing way that you know. He was interrupted by a loud scream from the girl, and then all was as still as death. Suddenly a loud racket was heard on the stairs; a young man rushed out sobbing, threw himself into a post-chaise which stood below, and drove rapidly away. The next day the Councillor was very cheerful, and nobody had the courage to question him about the events of the previous night. But on inquiring of the housekeeper, we gathered that the Councillor had brought home with him an extraordinarily pretty young lady whom he called Antonia, and she it was who had sung so beautifully. A young man also had come along with them; he had treated Antonia very tenderly, and must evidently have been her betrothed. But he, since the Councillor peremptorily insisted on it, had had to go away again in a hurry. What the relations between Antonia and the Councillor are has remained until now a secret, but this much is certain, that he tyrannizes over the poor girl in the most hateful fashion. He watches her as Doctor Bartholo watches his ward in the *Barber of Seville*; she hardly dare show herself at the window; and if, yielding now and again to her earnest entreaties, he takes her into society, he follows her with Argus' eyes, and will on no account suffer a musical note to be sounded, far less let Antonia sing – indeed, she is not permitted to sing in his own house. Antonia's singing on that memorable night has, therefore, come to be regarded by the townspeople in the light of a tradition of some marvellous wonder that suffices to stir the heart and the fancy; and even those who did not hear it often exclaim, whenever any other singer attempts to display her powers in the place, "What sort of a wretched squeaking do you call that? Nobody but Antonia knows how to sing." '

Having a singular weakness for such like fantastic histories, I found it necessary, as may easily be imagined, to make Antonia's acquaintance. I had myself often enough heard the popular sayings about her singing, but had never imagined that that exquisite *artiste* was living in the place, held a captive in the bonds of this eccentric Krespel like the victim of a tyrannous sorcerer. Naturally enough I heard in my dreams on the following night Antonia's marvellous voice, and as she besought me in the most touching manner in a glorious *adagio* movement (very ridiculously it seemed to me, as if I had composed it myself) to save her, I soon resolved, like a second Astolpho,* to penetrate into Krespel's house, as if into another Alcina's magic castle, and deliver the queen of song from her ignominious fetters.

It all came about in a different way from what I had expected; I had seen the Councillor scarcely more than two or three times,

* A reference to Ariosto's *Orlando Furioso*. Astolpho, an English cousin of Orlando, was a great boaster, but generous, courteous, gay, and remarkably handsome; he was carried to Alcina's island on the back of a whale.

and eagerly discussed with him the best method of constructing violins, when he invited me to call and see him. I did so; and he showed me his treasures of violins. There were fully thirty of them hanging up in a closet; one amongst them bore conspicuously all the marks of great antiquity (a carved lion's head, &c.), and, hung up higher than the rest and surmounted by a crown of flowers, it seemed to exercise a queenly supremacy over them. 'This violin,' said Krespel, on my making some inquiry relative to it, 'this violin is a very remarkable and curious specimen of the work of some unknown master, probably of Tartini's* age. I am perfectly convinced that there is something especially exceptional in its inner construction, and that, if I took it to pieces, a secret would be revealed to me which I have long been seeking to discover, but – laugh at me if you like – this senseless thing which only gives signs of life and sound as I make it, often speaks to me in a strange way of itself. The first time I played upon it I somehow fancied that I was only the magnetizer who has the power of moving his subject to reveal of his own accord in words the visions of his inner nature. Don't go away with the belief that I am such a fool as to attach even the slightest importance to such fantastic notions, and yet it's certainly strange that I could never prevail upon myself to cut open that dumb lifeless thing there. I am very pleased now that I have not cut it open, for since Antonia has been with me I sometimes play to her upon this violin. For Antonia is fond of it – very fond of it.' As the Councillor uttered these words with visible signs of emotion, I felt encouraged to hazard the question, 'Will you not play it to me, Councillor?' Krespel made a wry face, and falling into his drawling, singing way, said, 'No, my good sir!' and that was an end of the matter. Then I had to look at all sorts of rare curiosities, the greater

---

*Giuseppe Tartini, born in 1692, died in 1770; was one of the most celebrated violinists of the eighteenth century, and the discoverer (in 1714) of 'resultant tones,' or 'Tartini's tones' as they are frequently called. Most of his life was spent at Padua. He did much to advance the art of the violinist, both by his compositions for that instrument as well as by his treatise on its capabilities.

part of them childish trifles; at last thrusting his arm into a chest, he brought out a folded piece of paper, which he pressed into my hand, adding solemnly, 'You are a lover of art; take this present as a priceless memento, which you must value at all times above everything else.' Therewith he took me by the shoulders and gently pushed me towards the door, embracing me on the threshold. That is to say, I was in a symbolical manner virtually kicked out of doors. Unfolding the paper, I found a piece of a first string of a violin about an eighth of an inch in length, with the words, 'A piece of the treble string with which the deceased Stamitz* strung his violin for the last concert at which he ever played.'

This summary dismissal at mention of Antonia's name led me to infer that I should never see her; but I was mistaken, for on my second visit to the Councillor's I found her in his room, assisting him to put a violin together. At first sight Antonia did not make a strong impression; but soon I found it impossible to tear myself away from her blue eyes, her sweet rosy lips, her uncommonly graceful, lovely form. She was very pale; but a shrewd remark or a merry sally would call up a winning smile on her face and suffuse her cheeks with a deep burning flush, which, however, soon faded away to a faint rosy glow. My conversation with her was quite unconstrained, and yet I saw nothing whatever of the Argus-like watchings on Krespel's part which the Professor had imputed to him; on the contrary, his behaviour moved along the customary lines, nay, he even seemed to approve of my conversation with Antonia. So I often stepped in to see the Councillor; and as we became accustomed to each other's society, a singular feeling of homeliness, taking possession of our little circle of three, filled our hearts with inward happiness. I still continued to derive exquisite enjoyment from the Councillor's strange crotchets and oddities; but it was of course Antonia's irresistible charms alone which attracted me, and led me to put up with a good deal which I should other-

---

*This was the name of a well-known musical family from Bohemia. Karl Stamitz is the one here possibly meant, since he died about eighteen or twenty years previous to the publication of this tale.

wise, in the frame of mind in which I then was, have impatiently shunned. For it only too often happened that in the Councillor's characteristic extravagance there was mingled much that was dull and tiresome; and it was in a special degree irritating to me that, as often as I turned the conversation upon music, and particularly upon singing, he was sure to interrupt me, with that sardonic smile upon his face and those repulsive singing tones of his, by some remark of a quite opposite tendency, very often of a commonplace character. From the great distress which at such times Antonia's glances betrayed, I perceived that he only did it to deprive me of a pretext for calling upon her for a song. But I didn't relinquish my design. The hindrances which the Councillor threw in my way only strengthened my resolution to overcome them; I *must* hear Antonia sing if I was not to pine away in reveries and dim aspirations for want of hearing her.

One evening Krespel was in an uncommonly good humour; he had been taking an old Cremona violin to pieces, and had discovered that the sound-post was fixed half a line more obliquely than usual – an important discovery! one of incalculable advantage in the practical work of making violins! I succeeded in setting him off at full speed on his hobby of the true art of violin-playing. Mention of the way in which the old masters picked up their dexterity in execution from really great singers (which was what Krespel happened just then to be expatiating upon), naturally paved the way for the remark that now the practice was the exact opposite of this, the vocal score erroneously following the affected and abrupt transitions and rapid scaling of the instrumentalists. 'What is more nonsensical,' I cried, leaping from my chair, running to the piano, and opening it quickly, 'what is more nonsensical than such an execrable style as this, which, far from being music, is much more like the noise of peas rolling across the floor?' At the same time I sang several of the modern *fermatas*, which rush up and down and hum like a well-spun peg-top, striking a few villainous chords by way of accompaniment. Krespel laughed outrageously and screamed, 'Ha! ha! methinks I hear our German-Italians or

our Italian-Germans struggling with an aria from Pucitta,* or
Portogallo,† or some other *Maestro di capella*, or rather *schiavo
d'un primo uomo*.'‡ Now, thought I, now's the time; so turning
to Antonia, I remarked, 'Antonia knows nothing of such singing as that, I believe?' At the same time I struck up one of old
Leonardo Leo's§ beautiful soul-stirring songs. Then Antonia's
cheeks glowed: heavenly radiance sparkled in her eyes, which
grew full of reawakened inspiration; she hastened to the piano;
she opened her lips; but at that very moment Krespel pushed
her away, grasped me by the shoulders, and with a shriek that
rose up to a tenor pitch, cried, 'My son – my son – my son!'
And then he immediately went on, singing very softly, and
grasping my hand with a bow that was the pink of politeness,
'In very truth, my esteemed and honourable student-friend, in
very truth it would be a violation of the codes of social inter-
course, as well as of all good manners, were I to express aloud
and in a stirring way my wish that here, on this very spot, the
devil from hell would softly break your neck with his burning
claws, and so in a sense make short work of you; but, setting
that aside, you must acknowledge, my dearest friend, that it is
rapidly growing dark, and there are no lamps burning tonight,
so that, even though I did not kick you downstairs at once, your
darling limbs might still run a risk of suffering damage. Go
home by all means; and cherish a kind remembrance of your
faithful friend, if it should happen that you never, – pray, understand me, – if you should never see him in his own house again.'
Therewith he embraced me, and, still keeping fast hold of me,
turned with me slowly towards the door, so that I could not get

*Vincenzo Pucitta (1778–1861) was an Italian opera composer, whose
music 'shows great facility, but no invention'. He also wrote several songs.

†Il Portogallo was the Italian sobriquet of a Portuguese musician named
Mark Anthony Simão (1763–1829). He lived alternatively in Italy and
Portugal, and wrote several operas.

‡Literally, 'The slave of a *primo uomo*,' *primo uomo* being the
masculine form corresponding to *prima donna*, that is, a singer of hero's
parts in operatic music. At one time also female parts were sung and acted
by men or boys.

§Leonardo Leo, the chief Neapolitan representative of Italian music in
the first part of the eighteenth century, and author of more than forty
operas and nearly one hundred compositions for the Church.

another single look at Antonia. Of course it is plain enough that in my position I couldn't thrash the Councillor, though that is what he really deserved. The Professor enjoyed a good laugh at my expense, and assured me that I had ruined for ever all hopes of retaining the Councillor's friendship. Antonia was too dear to me, I might say too holy, for me to go and play the part of the languishing lover and stand gazing up at her window, or to fill the role of the love-sick adventurer. Completely upset, I went away from H—; but, as is usual in such cases, the brilliant colours of the picture of my fancy faded, and the recollection of Antonia, as well as of Antonia's singing (which I had never heard), often fell upon my heart like a soft faint trembling light, comforting me.

Two years afterwards I received an appointment in B—, and set out on a journey to the south of Germany. The towers of H— rose before me in the red vaporous glow of the evening; the nearer I came the more was I oppressed by an indescribable feeling of the most agonizing distress; it lay upon me like a heavy burden; I could not breathe; I was obliged to get out of my carriage into the open air. But my anguish continued to increase until it became actual physical pain. Soon I seemed to hear the strains of a solemn chorale floating in the air; the sounds continued to grow more distinct; I realized the fact that they were men's voices, chanting a church chorale. 'What's that? what's that?' I cried, a burning stab darting as it were through my breast. 'Don't you see?' replied the coachman, who was driving along beside me, 'why, don't you see? they're burying somebody up yonder in yon churchyard.' And indeed we were near the churchyard; I saw a circle of men clothed in black standing round a grave, which was on the point of being closed. Tears started to my eyes; I somehow fancied they were burying there all the joy and all the happiness of life. Moving on rapidly down the hill, I was no longer able to see into the churchyard; the chorale came to an end, and I perceived not far distant from the gate some of the mourners returning from the funeral. The Professor, with his niece on his arm, both in deep mourning, went close past me without noticing me. The young lady had her handkerchief pressed close to her eyes, and was weeping bitterly. In the frame of mind in which I then was I could not possibly go into the town, so I sent on my servant with the carriage to the hotel where I usually put up, whilst I took a turn in the familiar neighbourhood, to get rid of a mood that was possibly only due to physical causes, such as heating on the journey, &c. On arriving at a well-known avenue, which leads to a pleasure-resort, I came upon a most extraordinary spectacle. Councillor Krespel was being conducted by two mourners, from whom he appeared to be endeavouring to make his escape by all sorts of strange twists and turns. As usual, he was dressed in his own curious home-made grey coat; but from his little cocked-hat, which he wore perched over one ear in military fashion, a long narrow ribbon of black crape fluttered backwards and forwards in the wind. Around his waist he had buckled a black sword-belt; but instead of a sword he had stuck a long fiddle-bow into it. A creepy shudder ran through my limbs: 'He's insane,' thought I, as I slowly followed them. The Councillor's companions led him as far as his house, where he embraced them, laughing loudly. They left him; and then his glance fell upon me, for I now stood near him. He stared at me fixedly for some time; then he cried in a hollow voice, 'Welcome, my student-friend! you also understand it!' Therewith he took me by the arm and pulled me into the house, up the steps, into the room where the violins hung. They were all draped in black crape; the violin of the old master was missing; in its place was a cypress wreath. I knew what had happened. 'Antonia! Antonia!' I cried in inconsolable grief. The Councillor, with his arms crossed on his breast, stood beside me, as if turned into stone. I pointed to the cypress wreath. 'When she died,' said he in a very hoarse solemn voice, 'when she died, the soundpost of that violin broke into pieces with a ringing crack, and the sound-board was split from end to end. The faithful instrument could only live with her and in her; it lies beside her in the coffin, it has been buried with her.' Deeply agitated, I sank down upon a chair, whilst the Councillor began to sing a gay song in a husky voice; it was truly horrible to see him hopping about on one foot, and the crape strings (he still had his hat on) flying about the room and up to the violins hanging on the walls. Indeed, I could not repress a loud cry that rose to my lips when, on the Councillor making an abrupt turn, the crape came all over me; I fancied he wanted to envelop me in it and drag me down into the horrible dark depths of insanity. Suddenly he stood still and addressed me in his singing way, 'My son l my son l why do you call out? Have you espied the angel of death? That always precedes the ceremony.' Stepping into the middle of the room, he took the violin-bow out of his sword-belt, and, holding it over his head with both hands, broke it into a thousand pieces. Then, with a loud laugh, he cried, 'Now you imagine my sentence is pronounced, don't you, my son? but it's nothing of the kind – not at all l not at all l Now I'm free – free – free – hurrah l I'm free l Now I shall make no more violins – no more violins – Hurrah l no more violins l' This he sang to a horrible mirthful tune, again spinning round on one foot. Perfectly aghast, I was making the best of my way to the door, when he held me fast, saying quite calmly, 'Stay, my student friend, pray don't think from this outbreak of grief, which is torturing me as if with the agonies of death, that I am insane; I only do it because a short time ago I made myself a dressing-gown in which I wanted to look like Fate or like God l' The Councillor then went on with a medley of silly and awful rubbish, until he fell down utterly exhausted; I called up the old housekeeper, and was very pleased to find myself in the open air again.

I never doubted for a moment that Krespel had become insane; the Professor, however, asserted the contrary. 'There are men,' he remarked, 'from whom nature or a special destiny has taken away the cover behind which the mad folly of the rest of us runs its course unobserved. They are like thin-skinned insects, which, as we watch the restless play of their muscles, seem to be misshapen, while nevertheless everything soon comes back into its proper form again. All that with us remains thought, passes over with Krespel into action. That bitter scorn which the spirit that is wrapped up in the doings and dealings of the earth often has at hand, Krespel gives vent to in outrageous gestures and agile caprioles. But these are his lightning conductor. What comes up out of the earth he gives again to the earth, but what is divine, that he keeps; and so I believe that his inner conscious-ness, in spite of the apparent madness which springs from it to the surface, is as right as a trivet. To be sure, Antonia's sudden death grieves him sore, but I warrant that tomorrow will see him going along in his old jog-trot way as usual.' And the Pro-fessor's prediction was almost literally filled. Next day the Coun-cillor appeared to be just as he formerly was, only he averred that he would never make another violin, nor yet ever play on another. And, as I learned later, he kept his word.

Hints which the Professor let fall confirmed my own private conviction that the so carefully guarded secret of the Councillor's relations to Antonia, nay, that even her death, was a crime which must weigh heavily upon him, a crime that could not be atoned for. I determined that I would not leave H— without tax-ing him with the offence which I conceived him to be guilty of; I determined to shake his heart down to its very roots, and so compel him to make open confession of the terrible deed. The more I reflected upon the matter the clearer it grew in my own mind that Krespel must be a villain, and in the same propor-tion did my intended reproach, which assumed of itself the form of a real rhetorical masterpiece, wax more fiery and more im-pressive. Thus equipped and mightily incensed, I hurried to his house. I found him with a calm smiling countenance making playthings. 'How can peace,' I burst out, 'how can peace find lodgement even for a single moment in your breast, so long as the memory of your horrible deed preys like a serpent upon you?' He gazed at me in amazement, and laid his chisel aside. 'What do you mean, my dear sir?' he asked; 'pray take a seat.' But my indignation chafing me more and more, I went on to accuse him directly of having murdered Antonia, and to threaten him with the vengeance of the Eternal.

Further, as a newly full-fledged lawyer, full of my profession, I went so far as to give him to understand that I would leave no stone unturned to get a clue to the business, and so deliver him here in this world into the hands of an earthly judge. I must confess that I was considerably disconcerted when, at the conclusion of my violent and pompous harangue, the Councillor, without answering so much as a single word, calmly fixed his eyes upon me as though expecting me to go on again. And this I did indeed attempt to do, but it sounded so ill-founded and so stupid as well that I soon grew silent again. Krespel gloated over my embarrassment, whilst a malicious ironical smile flitted across his face. Then he grew very grave, and addressed me in solemn tones. 'Young man, no doubt you think I am foolish, insane; that I can pardon you, since we are both confined in the same madhouse; and you only blame me for deluding myself with the idea that I am God the Father because you imagine yourself to be God the Son. But how do you dare desire to insinuate yourself into the secrets and lay bare the hidden motives of a life that is strange to you and that must continue so? She has gone and the mystery is solved.' He ceased speaking, rose, and traversed the room backwards and forwards several times. I ventured to ask for an explanation; he fixed his eyes upon me, grasped me by the hand, and led me to the window, which he threw wide open. Propping himself upon his arms, he leaned out, and looking down into the garden, told me the history of his life. When he finished I left him, touched and ashamed.

In a few words, his relations with Antonia rose in the following way. Twenty years before, the Councillor had been led into Italy by his favourite engrossing passion of hunting up and buying the best violins of the old masters. At that time he had not yet begun to make them himself, and so of course he had not begun to take to pieces those which he bought. In Venice he heard the celebrated singer Angela —i, who at that time was playing with splendid success as *prima donna* at St Benedict's Theatre. His enthusiasm was awakened, not only in her art – which Signora Angela had indeed brought to a high pitch of perfection – but in her angelic beauty as well. He sought her acquaintance; and in spite of all his rugged manners he succeeded in winning her heart, principally through his bold and yet at the same time masterly violin-playing. Close intimacy led in a few weeks to marriage, which, however, was kept a secret, because

Angela was unwilling to sever her connection with the theatre, neither did she wish to part with her professional name, that by which she was celebrated, nor to add to it the cacophonous 'Krespel.' With the most extravagant irony he described to me what a strange life of worry and torture Angela led him as soon as she became his wife. Krespel was of opinion that more capriciousness and waywardness were concentrated in Angela's little person than in all the rest of the *prima donnas* in the world put together. If he now and again presumed to stand up in his own defence, she let loose a whole army of abbots, musical composers, and students upon him, who, ignorant of his true connection with Angela, soundly rated him as a most intolerable, ungallant lover for not submitting to all the Signora's caprices. It was just after one of these stormy scenes that Krespel fled to Angela's country seat to try and forget in playing fantasias on his Cremona violin the annoyances of the day. But he had not been there long before the Signora, who had followed hard after him, stepped into the room. She was in an affectionate humour; she embraced her husband, overwhelmed him with sweet and languishing glances, and rested her pretty head on his shoulder. But Krespel, carried away into the world of music, continued to play on until the walls echoed again; thus he chanced to touch the Signora somewhat ungently with his arm and the fiddle-bow. She leapt back full of fury, shrieking that he was a 'German brute,' snatched the violin from his hands, and dashed it on the marble table into a thousand pieces. Krespel stood like a statue of stone before her; but then, as if awakening out of a dream, he seized her with the strength of a giant and threw her out of the window of her own house, and, without troubling himself about anything more, fled back to Venice – to Germany. It was not, however, until some time had elapsed that he had a clear recollection of what he had done; although he knew that the window was scarcely five feet from the ground, and although he was fully cognizant of the necessity, under the above-mentioned circumstances, of throwing the Signora out of the window, he yet felt troubled by a sense of painful uneasiness, and the more so since she had imparted to him in no

ambiguous terms an interesting secret as to her condition. He
hardly dared to make inquiries; and he was not a little surprised
about eight months afterwards at receiving a tender letter from
his beloved wife, in which she made not the slightest allusion to
what had taken place in her country house, only adding to the
intelligence that she had been safely delivered of a sweet little
daughter the heartfelt prayer that her dear husband and now a
happy father would come at once to Venice. That however
Krespel did not do; rather he appealed to a confidential friend
for a more circumstantial account of the details, and learned
that the Signora had alighted upon the soft grass as lightly as a
bird, and that the sole consequences of the fall or shock had
been psychic. That is to say, after Krespel's heroic deed she had
become completely altered; she never showed a trace of caprice,
of her former freaks, or of her teasing habits; and the composer
who wrote for the next carnival was the happiest fellow under
the sun, since the Signora was willing to sing his music without
the scores and hundreds of changes which she at other times had
insisted upon. 'To be sure,' added his friend, 'there was every
reason for preserving the secret of Angela's cure, else every day
would see lady singers flying through windows.' The Councillor was not a little excited at this news; he engaged horses; he
took his seat in the carriage. 'Stop!' he cried suddenly. 'Why,
there's not a shadow of doubt,' he murmured to himself, 'that
as soon as Angela sets eyes upon me again the evil spirit will
recover his power and once more take possession of her. And
since I have already thrown her out of the window, what could
I do if a similar case were to occur again? What would there
be left for me to do?' He got out of the carriage, and wrote an
affectionate letter to his wife, making graceful allusion to her
tenderness in especially dwelling upon the fact that his tiny
daughter had like him a little mole behind the ear, and – remained in Germany. Now ensued an active correspondence between them. Assurances of unchanged affection – invitations
– laments over the absence of the beloved one – thwarted wishes
– hopes, &c. – flew backwards and forwards from Venice to
H—, from H— to Venice. At length Angela came to Germany,

and as is well known, sang with brilliant success as *prima donna* at the great theatre in F—. Despite the fact that she was no longer young, she won all hearts by the irresistible charm of her wonderfully splendid singing. At that time she had not lost her voice in the least degree. Meanwhile, Antonia had been growing up; and her mother never tired of writing to tell her father how that a singer of the first rank was developing in her. Krespel's friends in F— also confirmed this intelligence, and urged him to come for once to F— to see and admire this uncommon sight of two such glorious singers. They had not the slightest suspicion of the close relations in which Krespel stood to the pair. Willingly would he have seen with his own eyes the daughter who occupied so large a place in his heart, and who moreover often appeared to him in his dreams; but as often as he thought upon his wife he felt very uncomfortable, and so he remained at home amongst his broken violins.

There was a certain promising young composer, B— of F—, who was found to have suddenly disappeared, nobody knew where. This young man fell so deeply in love with Antonia that, as she returned his love, he earnestly besought her mother to consent to an immediate union, sanctified as it would further be by art. Angela had nothing to urge against his suit; and the Councillor the more readily gave his consent that the young composer's productions had found favour before his rigorous critical judgement. Krespel was expecting to hear of the consummation of the marriage, when he received instead a black-sealed envelope addressed in a strange hand. Doctor R— conveyed to the Councillor the sad intelligence that Angela had fallen seriously ill in consequence of a cold caught at the theatre, and that during the night immediately preceding what was to have been Antonia's wedding-day, she had died. To him, the Doctor, Angela had disclosed the fact that she was Krespel's wife, and that Antonia was his daughter; he, Krespel, had better hasten therefore to take charge of the orphan. Notwithstanding that the Councillor was a good deal upset by this news of Angela's death, he soon began to feel that an antipathetic, disturbing influence had departed out of his life, and that now for the first time he could begin to breathe freely. The very same day he set out for F—. You could not credit how heartrending was the Councillor's description of the moment when he first saw Antonia. Even in the fantastic oddities of his expression there was such a marvellous power of description that I am unable to give even so much as a faint indication of it. Antonia inherited all her mother's amiability and all her mother's charms, but not the repellent reverse of the medal. There was no chronic moral ulcer, which might break out from time to time. Antonia's betrothed put in an appearance, whilst Antonia herself, fathoming with happy instinct the deeper-lying character of her wonderful father, sang one of old Padre Martini's* motets, which, she knew, Krespel in the heyday of his courtship had never grown tired of hearing her mother sing. The tears ran in streams down Krespel's cheeks; even Angela he had never heard sing like that. Antonia's voice was of a very remarkable and altogether peculiar timbre, at one time it was like the sighing of an Æolian harp, at another like the warbled gush of the nightingale. It seemed as if there was not room for such notes in the human breast. Antonia, blushing with joy and happiness, sang on and on – all her most beautiful songs, B— playing between whiles as only enthusiasm that is intoxicated with delight can play. Krespel was at first transported with rapture, then he grew thoughtful – still – absorbed in reflection. At length he leapt to his feet, pressed Antonia to his heart, and begged her in a low husky voice, 'Sing no more if you love me – my heart is bursting – I fear – I fear – don't sing again.'

'No!' remarked the Councillor next day to Doctor R—, 'when, as she sang, her blushes gathered into two dark red spots on her pale cheeks, I knew it had nothing to do with your nonsensical family likenesses, I knew it was what I dreaded.' The Doctor, whose countenance had shown signs of deep distress

*Giambattista Martini, more commonly called Padre Martini, of Bologna, formed an influential school of music there in the latter half of the eighteenth century. He wrote vocal and instrumental pieces both for the church and for the theatre. He was also a learned historian of music. He has the merit of having discerned and encouraged the genius of Mozart when, a boy of fourteen, he visited Bologna in 1770.

from the very beginning of the conversation, replied, 'Whether it arises from a too early taxing of her powers of song, or whether the fault is Nature's – enough, Antonia labours under an organic failure in the chest, while it is from it too that her voice derives its wonderful power and its singular timbre, which I might almost say transcend the limits of human capabilities of song. But it bears the announcement of her early death; for, if she continues to sing, I wouldn't give her at the most more than six months longer to live.' Krespel's heart was lacerated as if by the stabs of hundreds of stinging knives. It was as though his life had been for the first time overshadowed by a beautiful tree full of the most magnificent blossoms, and now it was to be sawn to pieces at the roots, so that it could not grow green and blossom any more. His resolution was taken. He told Antonia all; he put the alternatives before her – whether she would follow her betrothed and yield to his and the world's seductions, but with the certainty of dying early, or whether she would spread round her father in his old days that joy and peace which had hitherto been unknown to him, and so secure a long life. She threw herself sobbing into his arms, and he, knowing the heartrending trial that was before her, did not press for a more explicit declaration. He talked the matter over with her betrothed; but, notwithstanding that the latter averred that no note should ever cross Antonia's lips, the Councillor was only too well aware that even B— could not resist the temptation of hearing her sing, at any rate arias of his own composition. And the world, the musical public, even though acquainted with the nature of the singer's affliction, would certainly not relinquish its claims to hear her, for in cases where pleasure is concerned people of this class are very selfish and cruel. The Councillor disappeared from F— along with Antonia, and came to H—. B— was in despair when he learnt that they had gone. He set out on their track, overtook them, and arrived at H— at the same time that they did. 'Let me see him only once, and then die!' entreated Antonia. 'Die! die!' cried Krespel, wild with anger, an icy shudder running through him. His daughter, the only creature in the wide world who had awakened in him the springs of unknown joy, who alone had reconciled him to life, tore herself away from his heart, and he – he suffered the terrible trial to take place. B— sat down to the piano; Antonia sang; Krespel fiddled away merrily, until the two red spots showed themselves on Antonia's cheeks. Then he bade her stop; and as B— was taking leave of his betrothed, she suddenly fell to the floor with a loud scream. 'I thought,' continued Krespel in his narration, 'I thought that she was, as I had anticipated, really dead; but as I had prepared myself for the worst, my calmness did not leave me, nor my self-command desert me. I grasped B—, who stood like a silly sheep in his dismay, by the shoulders, and said (here the Councillor fell into his singing tone), "Now that you, my estimable pianoforte-player, have, as you wished and desired, really murdered your betrothed, you may quietly take your departure; at least have the goodness to make yourself scarce before I run my bright hanger through your heart. My daughter, who, as you see, is rather pale, could very well do with some colour from your precious blood. Make haste and run, for I might also hurl a nimble knife or two after you." I must, I suppose, have looked rather formidable as I uttered these words, for, with a cry of the greatest terror, B— tore himself loose from my grasp, rushed out of the room, and down the steps.' Directly after B— was gone, when the Councillor tried to lift up his daughter, who lay unconscious on the floor, she opened her eyes with a deep sigh, but soon closed them again as if about to die. Then Krespel's grief found vent aloud, and would not be comforted. The Doctor, whom the old house-keeper had called in, pronounced Antonia's case a somewhat serious but by no means dangerous attack; and she did indeed recover more quickly than her father had dared to hope. She now clung to him with the most confiding childlike affection; she entered into his favourite hobbies – into his mad schemes and whims. She helped him take old violins to pieces and glue new ones together. 'I won't sing again any more, but live for you,' she often said, sweetly smiling upon him, after she had been asked to sing and had refused. Such appeals however the Councillor was anxious to spare her as much as possible; there-

fore it was that he was unwilling to take her into society, and
solicitously shunned all music. He well understood how painful
it must be for her to forego altogether the exercise of that art
which she had brought to such a pitch of perfection. When the
Councillor bought the wonderful violin that he had buried with
Antonia, and was about to take it to pieces, she met him with
such sadness in her face and softly breathed the petition, 'What!
this as well?' By some power, which he could not explain, he
felt impelled to leave this particular instrument unbroken, and
to play upon it. Scarcely had he drawn the first few notes from it
than Antonia cried aloud with joy, 'Why, that's me! – now I
shall sing again.' And, in truth, there was something remarkably striking about the clear, silvery, bell-like tones of the violin;
they seemed to have been engendered in the human soul. Krespel's heart was deeply moved; he played, too, better than ever. As
he ran up and down the scale, playing bold passages with con-
summate power and expression, she clapped her hands together
and cried with delight, 'I did that well! I did that well!'

From this time onwards her life was filled with peace and
cheerfulness. She often said to the Councillor, 'I should like to
sing something, father.' Then Krespel would take his violin
down from the wall and play her most beautiful songs, and her
heart was right glad and happy. Shortly before my arrival in
H—, the Councillor fancied one night that he heard somebody
playing the piano in the adjoining room, and he soon made out
distinctly that B— was flourishing on the instrument in his usual
style. He wished to get up, but felt himself held down as if by a
dead weight, and lying as if fettered in iron bonds; he was utterly unable to move an inch. Then Antonia's voice was heard
singing low and soft; soon, however, it began to rise and rise in
volume until it became an ear-splitting *fortissimo*; and at length
she passed over into a powerfully impressive song which B—
had once composed for her in the devotional style of the old
masters. Krespel described his condition as being incomprehen-
sible, for terrible anguish was mingled with a delight he had
never experienced before. All at once he was surrounded by a
dazzling brightness, in which he beheld B— and Antonia locked

in a close embrace, and gazing at each other in a rapture of ecstacy. The music of the song and of the pianoforte accompanying it went on without any visible signs that Antonia sang or that B— touched the instrument. Then the Councillor fell into a sort of dead faint, whilst the images vanished away. On awakening he still felt the terrible anguish of his dream. He rushed into Antonia's room. She lay on the sofa, her eyes closed, a sweet angelic smile on her face, her hands devoutly folded, and looking as if asleep and dreaming of the joys and raptures of heaven. But she was – dead.